Cinderella

Retold by Patricia Whitten
Illustrated by Colin Petty

GALLERY BOOKS
An Imprint of W. H. Smith Publishers Inc.
112 Madison Avenue
New York City 10016

Once upon a time there was a good and
beautiful girl who lived with her stepmother
and two selfish and ugly stepsisters.

The stepmother dressed the girl in rags and

made her scrub and clean all day. At night the girl
slept near the cinders in the fireplace to keep warm
so everyone called her Cinderella.

One day a royal messenger arrived with
invitations to a dance being given by the Prince.
"Can I go to the dance, too?" asked Cinderella.
"Don't be silly," laughed her stepmother.
"What would you wear? Your rags?"

On the night of the dance, Cinderella watched sadly as her stepmother and stepsisters left to meet the Prince.

"I wish I could go to the dance," sobbed poor Cinderella.

"You shall go to the dance," a soft voice said.

Cinderella looked up in surprise and saw a kindly lady holding a silver wand.

"I am your fairy godmother," the lady said. "Go to the garden and bring me a large pumpkin and the mousetrap with six plump mice."

When Cinderella returned, her fairy godmother waved her wand and Cinderella's rags became a beautiful dress, and there were two shining glass slippers on her feet.

With another wave of her wand, Cinderella's
godmother turned the pumpkin into a beautiful
gold coach and the mice into six prancing horses.
While Cinderella was climbing into the coach,

her fairy godmother called out a warning to the
happy girl.

"You must be home by midnight. When the
clock strikes twelve, the spell will be broken."

When Cinderella arrived at the dance, people whispered, "Who is that beautiful girl?" but no one knew, not even her stepmother or stepsisters.

The Prince thought Cinderella was the most beautiful girl he had ever met. They danced and danced.

Cinderella had such a wonderful time
dancing with the Prince that she forgot her
fairy godmother's warning.

Suddenly the clock began to strike twelve.
Cinderella gasped and ran out of the room so
quickly that she lost one of her glass slippers.

When the Prince got to the door, there was no
sign of Cinderella. He picked up the glass slipper
and decided to find the girl who had lost the
slipper.

The Prince traveled all over the kingdom
looking for Cinderella. One day he arrived at
Cinderella's house. The two ugly stepsisters
pushed and pulled, trying to make the glass slipper
fit. But it was no use.

Then the Prince saw Cinderella curled up by the fireplace.

"Would you like to try on the slipper?" he asked kindly.

The Prince knelt down and put the glass slipper on Cinderella's foot. It was a perfect fit!

The Prince was overjoyed. And when he asked Cinderella to marry him, of course she said, "Yes!"

When Cinderella and her Prince were married, all the people in the kingdom rejoiced. And Cinderella and the Prince lived happily ever after.